libraries

Ibrox Library
1 Midlock Stre
Glasgow G51 1
Phone: 0141 27

This book is due for return on or before the last date shown below. It may
be renewed by telephone, personal application, fax or post, quoting this
date, author, title and the book number

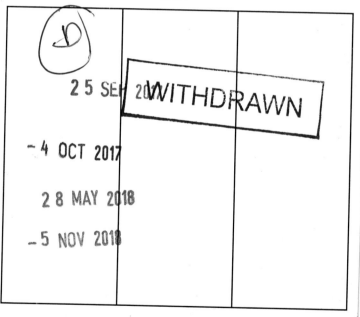

25 SEP 20~ WITHDRAWN

~4 OCT 2017

28 MAY 2018

~5 NOV 2018

Glasgow Life and its service brands, including Glasgow
Libraries, (found at www.glasgowlife.org.uk) are operating
names for Culture and Sport Glasgow

 Glasgow
CITY COUNCIL

For Iona: dream big, little one – D.S.

To my godson Anthony: I'm so proud of what a
wonderful grown-up you've become! – A.A.M.

Young Kelpies is an imprint of Floris Books
First published in 2016 by Floris Books

The publisher acknowledges subsidy from
Creative Scotland towards the publication
of this volume

MIX
Paper from
responsible sources
FSC® C007785
www.fsc.org

This book is also
available as an eBook

British Library CIP data available
ISBN 978-178250-281-4
Printed in Great Britain by Bell & Bain Ltd

CALUM'S TOUGH MATCH

written by **Danny Scott**

illustrated by **Alice A. Morentorn**

Young
Kelpies

ERIKA
BROWN

CALUM
FERGUSON

LEIGHTON

LEO
NKWANU

King's Park Athletic

Jordan's house

Caleytown shopping centre

Fraser's house

Park

Leo's house

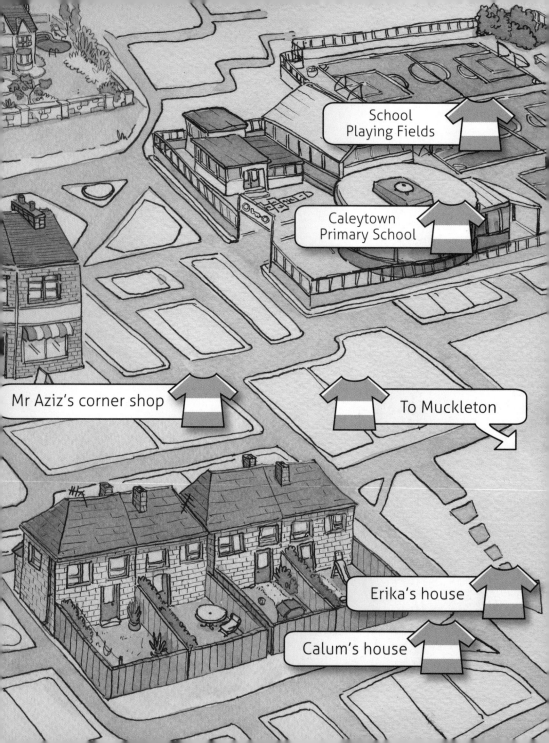

The Playoffs Beckon

Everything was going perfectly. Caleytown Primary were leading St Catherine's 3–1. The playoffs beckoned.

"St Catherine's are history. Bring on Muckleton!" Calum's best friend Leo Nkwanu shouted across from out on the left wing.

Calum didn't respond. He knew they'd soon be facing their biggest rivals in a crucial playoff, but he wasn't done with this match just yet. He watched as their captain, the classy

Janek Powolski, stopped a rare St Catherine's attack dead in its tracks. Everybody moved into position like clockwork.

"Let's finish this, gentlemen," shouted Caleytown's coach and Calum's teacher, Mr McKlop.

Lewis Budge, the busy red-haired midfielder, dropped back to form a neat triangle with Janek and Jordan McPride in defence.

"Centre it, big man!" he shouted.

Janek did, and Lewis spun and found Calum with a pass. Caleytown's number nine knew instinctively where Leo would be and side-footed a one-touch pass out to the wing.

"Great stuff, gentlemen. " Mr McKlop clapped as his floppy brown hair blew down over his glasses.

Leo dribbled forward with his yellow Caleytown strip flapping and his socks round his ankles. He flicked a pass back to Calum, who took a touch before finding their zippy P5 friend Fraser McDonald on the right.

Fraser's cartoon-like blue eyes tracked Leo's run across the box as if he were a dot on a radar.

"Hit me with it, Frazzler!" Leo shouted.

Calum stopped for a moment in the icy February wind to see what Fraser would do. A round

St Catherine's defender moved over to eclipse Leo, so Fraser went it alone.

He danced in off the right wing to fire a shot at the St Catherine's goal.

The keeper could do nothing but deflect the ball with his knees, straight to Calum's feet.

"Finish it, Cal!" Fraser shrieked.

But Calum didn't panic. The game was already won. The pressure was off. He took a touch, positioned his yellow boots and smashed the ball into the far bottom corner to make it 4–1. Game over. Caleytown had come a long way since their embarrassing loss, and recent team meltdown, at home to Battlehill.

The whistle sounded shortly after, and all

three subs poured onto the pitch from the sideline.

Calum saw their keeper Ravi, rocketing up the pitch to join them. "Nice goal, Calum! Playoffs here we come!"

Ravi launched himself into the big yellow huddle and the low winter sun cast their long shadows on the frosty ground.

"In sport news, our P6 boys have made it to the Scotland Stars Soccer Sevens playoffs!" Headteacher Sanderson announced to the older half of the school at assembly. "Come up here, lads."

Calum and his teammates sloped up to the stage. They all had their hands in their pockets and were looking at the ground – apart from Jordan, who'd popped his collar up, and Ravi, who was pointing and waving to his pals.

"Our footballing stars will now play our neighbours – and some say rivals – Muckleton Primary, in a two-legged playoff, home and away. Should they win, they will go on to compete in the *National* Soccer Sevens Tournament at Heroes Glen Indoor Arena." The headteacher held the paper Mr McKlop had given her like she was suspicious of it. "Please give them a Caleytown roar for their achievements!"

Mrs Brown, the American coach of the P6 girls' team, went crazy, punching the air and whooping. Calum searched the rows of pupils for her daughter, his next-door neighbour Erika Brown. She was sitting next

to her friend Sally Stewart, hiding her face, embarrassed about her mum's lack of volume control.

Instead of clapping, the P7 boys' team made farting noises with their hands. They hadn't made the playoffs last year. It was a sore point.

Headteacher Sanderson waited for silence before she continued. "I am all too aware of the long tradition of playoff pranks between our school and Muckleton," she whispered, her pointy nose aimed at the team like an extra finger in the middle of her face. "If I hear of any nonsense in relation to this year's matches I won't hesitate to forfeit the tie."

There was a gasp as the upper school realised what was at stake. After assembly, it was all anyone could talk about.

As Calum made his way to class with Leo and Jordan, the P7s appeared at their shoulders.

You lot better have something planned.

Forget what Sanderson said.

Don't chicken out!

"Erm, yeah." Jordan fiddled with his collar. "Course we've got something planned!"

"Have we?" Calum whispered to Jordan, as they turned away from the P7s and into Mr McKlop's classroom.

Jordan ignored him.

Calum turned to Leo and raised his eyebrow. "It's news to me."

Scotland Stars Preview

The next night, Calum was round at Leo's with an uncomfortable belly full of his mum's legendary spaghetti bolognaise. He'd eaten more than he thought possible – even Leo was impressed, and Leo could eat.

They'd managed to bargain with Leo's little sister Anya to get the family's tablet for half an hour. They went straight to the Scotland Stars website to watch the new report on Muckleton.

Leo tapped on reporter Reiss Robertson's face to start the video.

Robertson spun round to face three Muckleton players. Calum recognised two of them from his first ever game for Caleytown, and from their recent draw in the league. But he hadn't met Muckleton's keeper, who had only moved to the town halfway through the school year.

> I'm here with Muckleton captain Jack Stark, the league's top scorer Kyle Barclay and highly rated stopper Tom Tsang.

All three players wore black school blazers, only Tom Tsang had his goalie gloves on, too. It was rumoured that he wore them all the

time so they would feel like his actual hands during matches.

"They look like dorks with their blazers on," Leo snorted.

Calum tried to shush him but, with his full belly, his shush turned into a burp.

"Gross, Cal," Leo said. "That was right in my face!"

"Sorry, dude." Calum reached over Leo to turn the volume up.

Reiss Robertson raised an eyebrow and continued. "Ah yes, the famous Caleytown – Muckleton rivalry. Can we expect the usual pre-match pranks and practical jokes?"

Tom Tsang scratched his nose with his goalie glove to hide his face.

Jack Stark wasn't so shy. He looked at the camera and smirked. "No comment."

Jumpers
for Goalposts

That Saturday, the team met up without
Mr McKlop in Caleytown's public park to train
before their first leg away against Muckleton.
Everyone was there except Fraser. The park was
near Calum's house, so his parents let him take
his dog Leighton along.

Instead of passing drills and all the other
stuff Mr McKlop usually made them do,
the squad decided just to play doubles.
After a few tournaments, Leo and Calum

finally managed to wangle the teams so they got to play together. It gave them both an energy boost.

"Let's show this lot how to play football!" Leo grinned.

Ravi kicked the ball into play. Leo barged his way on to it and chested a pass to Calum.

Calum controlled the ball and rolled round Lewis in one movement. He pinged a grasscutter shot at goal. The ball flew in past Ravi's outstretched leg and skiffed Leo's jacket, which was doubling as the right post.

Leighton barked in celebration and jumped up on his hind legs. The ball wedged itself under Jordan's bike.

"YES!" Calum ran over to Leo to bump fists. He only needed one more goal to go through to the next round of their mini-tournament. They made their way to stand next to the bikes.

"No way was that a goal, Cal!" Jordan halted him and Leo in their tracks. "It totally hit the post!"

Calum stared up at the grey sky like it had sent Jordan down to earth to make his life difficult. Despite the team's successes, it seemed Jordan would never stop winding Calum and Leo up.

"Come on, Jordan! If Leo's jacket was an actual post the ball would've gone in."

"*You're* a post if you think that's a goal," Jordan said, nudging Lewis.

Lewis fake-laughed but didn't seem too bothered about the dispute.

"Rules are rules: if the ball touches a jacket on its way in, it's not a goal." Jordan wasn't finished. "My dad says rules are important, and he should know because he—"

"We *all* know he used to play for King's Park Athletic," an unfamiliar voice interrupted the debate. "Give up, Jordan McPants! That was totally a goal."

Caleytown's P6 team all turned around to see two older boys sitting on their bikes, watching them. Calum recognised the one who had spoken as Ravi's older brother, Vikram. He was in

second year at the local high school.

The other guy was taller than Vik, had a trendy red winter jacket on, thick blond hair shaved at the sides and blue-green eyes that twinkled like marbles.

"What do you want, Vik?" Jordan asked his friend's older brother. His collar seemed to flop down like soggy cardboard.

"Don't get your McPants in a McTwist, *Jordi*."

Jordan opened his mouth to defend himself but thought better of it.

Calum and Leo smiled at each other. They enjoyed every moment of Jordan getting teased.

"Mind if we join in... Calum, isn't it?" Vik's friend asked Calum. "I'm Zack, by the way."

"Er... well, it's not my ball," Calum said. "It's Jordan's."

"No worries. Jordi won't mind," said Zack. "So, Calum... Ravi here has told us that you and Leo are the stars of the team. We're here to see if that's true."

"Stars of the team?" Jordan hissed. His red-hot eyes fixed on Ravi.

"Haven't you got any friends your own size, Vik?" Ravi quickly changed the subject.

"No, *Ravi*, let your brother play," said Jordan. He flipped his collar up so hard he almost ripped it clean off. "I'll show them who the star of this team is."

Janek took a long thoughtful look at Zack and Vik before speaking. "I'm going to head off."

"Me too," said Max.

Ewan and Ryan followed their captain's lead as well, leaving only Calum, Leo, Lewis, Ravi and Jordan.

"Fair enough," said Zack. "Looks like we'll have to play trebles. I'll go with Calum and Leo. Vik, you're with McPants and Lewis."

After Zack's compliment, Calum and Leo were desperate to show off their skills.

"Let's do this!" Leo shouted.

Ravi went to collect the ball, while Leighton kept his eyes fixed on Zack. He let out a low growl.

Pranking Muckleton

Calum enjoyed playing football with the older boys. He couldn't wait until he could shoot as hard as Zack, or run as fast as him.

Zack could also do a great dummy move: he would fake a shot with one foot, only to flick the ball to the side of his opponent and shoot with the other. It was so convincing that everyone fell for it more than once. Even Vik, who must have seen it loads of times before.

Desperate to impress, Jordan had been

paying close attention to Zack's moves. The defender squared up to Zack, fully expecting his dummy move. When Zack drew his right foot back to shoot, Jordan slid to block the expected shot from his left.

Embarrassingly for Jordan, he slid way too soon. Zack aborted his move and snorted at the sight of his marker diving out the way.

"Way to go, McPants," Vik panted after Zack blasted a fifth goal past Ravi. It wrapped up a win for his, Calum and Leo's team.

"It's McPRIDE, not McPants!" Jordan thumped the ground with his fist.

Zack's shot had sailed over the bikes and into some bushes next to the play-park.

"I'm not getting that," said Ravi.

"Yes you are." Vikram tried to get his breath back. "You've not even done any running."

"Whatever, guys, let's chill for a bit instead." Zack cracked open a smile. "I want to hear what you guys have in store for Mucklebum."

"We don't know yet," Calum started.

"Our coach, Mr McKlop, likes to pick the team just before kick off."

"*Alright.*" Zack rolled his eyes. "But I *meant* what *pranks* do you have in store?"

"When we were in P6 our keeper burst stink bombs in Muckleton's box just before half-time," Vik chimed in. "Their keeper had turned totally green by the end of the match."

"Eugh," Ravi said. "Why would you do that? You'd smell it when you were in attack as well!"

A horn tooted from the side of the park. A small truck sat idling by the kerb.

"That's my dad." Lewis jumped up and grabbed his bike. "Let me ken if we're playing tomorrow, Jordan."

Jordan nodded.

Lewis, who lived on a small farm just outside Caleytown, cycled the short distance to the road and threw his bike into the back of the truck. He waved as his dad drove away.

Jordan was fingering his collar. "We just haven't planned anything *yet*."

"No way!" Zack smiled. He looked at Calum. "You guys have got to do *something*. It's tradition!"

"Do we?" Leo asked. "Can't we just, like, beat them at football?"

"It's all the same thing," Zack said. "It'll help you get the upper hand... mentally."

Calum considered this. He'd heard pundits on football shows talking about managers'

mind games. Maybe big clubs did pranks on each other too.

"I have a plan," said Zack, glancing at their bikes on the ground. "We could all cycle to Muckleton tomorrow and do a prank at their school!"

Leo shook his head. "I can't leave town without my parents, I'd get grounded until high school."

"Yeah, plus Headteacher Sanderson said she'd take us out of the playoffs if she heard of any pranks," Calum said.

"Sandy wouldn't have the guts. Besides, no one needs to know," Zack said. "It's only fifteen minutes away, and you'll be with me and Vik the whole time."

Calum and Leo looked at each other. Neither of them wanted to lose face in front of the older boys, but they both knew the consequences if they got caught.

"James Cauldfield did it, back in the day," Zack added.

Calum's ears pricked up at the sound of his hero's name. James Cauldfield was the star striker at King's Park Athletic, the team they all supported. He'd gone to Caleytown Primary and even come to watch Calum and Leo play earlier in the season.

"What prank did he do?" Calum asked.

Leighton growled at Zack as he walked over to the bikes to grab his phone. He loaded an interview with James Cauldfield and turned up the volume.

Calum leaned in. He liked to absorb every word that came out of James Cauldfield's mouth.

So, James Cauldfield, what do you think King's Park Athletic needs in order to win more titles?

A rival. We don't have a big rival pushing us to be better. Barcelona has Real Madrid, Manchester United has Manchester City. Even at my primary school, Caleytown, we had another local school, Muckleton. We'd play pranks on each other to get the upper hand. Anything to win, right?

Zack clicked his screen off and looked down at the younger boys. "Shall we meet here tomorrow morning then?"

Leighton growled. Calum held out a hand to quieten him. He looked at Leo. They both shrugged.

"Alright."

Tangled Webs

"Yes!" Calum whispered as he finally found some yellow wool in the cupboard under the stairs the next morning. Like a bank robber, he shovelled it into his rucksack with the white wool he'd already collected. Then he zipped his bag up and closed the door quietly.

His mum was standing behind it.

"What exactly are you doing, Cal?" she asked, stifling a yawn. Even the freckles on her cheeks looked sleepy.

43

Calum looked down at his bag then back at his mum's tired face. "Uhhh... Leo's mum has been teaching him how to knit... it's really cool... it's... er... good for hand-eye coordination."

"*Right.* That's great, love, but were you going to ask before you took my good wool for your... knitting with Leo?" His mum looked like she thought she might be dreaming.

"Sorry, Mu—" Calum was interrupted by the sound of a phone buzzing in his mum's dressing-gown pocket.

"For goodness' sake." Her hands were full. "See who that is, would you, Cal?"

Calum reached in and grabbed the phone. The display showed his dad's face.

45

"Dad?" Calum answered.

"Oh, hi Cal." Calum heard his dad's voice both in the phone and upstairs at the same time. "Could you ask your mum to bring some biscuits too, please?"

"Hang up on him," Calum's mum said in mock outrage and turned to go back to the kitchen. "Don't use all my wool – and be back by lunchtime!"

"I won't – I will," Calum lied, twice.

"How's Scotland's future number nine?" Mr Aziz's bushy moustache curved into a smile as

Calum walked into his local shop. Mr Aziz was wearing, a woolly cardigan and had a heater on behind the counter. When he saw Leo too, he added, "And Scotland's future winger!"

The boys had left their bikes outside to get snacks for the adventure ahead.

Mr Aziz turned the TV volume down. He was watching a programme about the weekend's matches so far: King's Park Athletic had lost at home to Aberdeen, leaving them in fourth, way off the top.

"It's looking like a disappointing season," Mr Aziz sighed. "At least you boys can provide some local success! How are your preparations for Muckleton going?"

47

For a moment, Calum didn't know if Mr Aziz was talking about the pranks or the upcoming match. His insides felt like a heavy cake-mix of guilt and excitement.

"Great, Mr Aziz," Leo answered for both of them. "Everyone has them as favourites but we've already beaten them in a friendly this year. Plus, we drew in the league, so we'll tonk them now!"

"I like your confidence," Mr Aziz chuckled as he rang their snacks through the till.

The boys opened their bags to stuff them in, revealing several balls of wool inside.

Mr Aziz raised an eyebrow. "Got big knitting plans for today, hey?"

"Er, kind of! Coach McKlop says doing cat's cradle is good for concentration," Leo lied.

"Ah, ok," said Mr Aziz. He smiled like a man who'd heard, and probably seen, it all before.

Calum stood, frozen with guilt, but Leo pulled him by his hood towards the shop door. Outside, the boys literally bumped into Calum's neighbour Erika.

49

"Hey, watch where you're going!" Erika's bushy ponytail flipped left and right as she looked at Calum and Leo in their hoodies, with full rucksacks. "Hang on, where *are* you going?"

"To do the biggest cat's cradle in the world on Muckleton's goals," Leo boasted.

"*Leo!*" Calum was surprised at his friend's lack of caution. Erika's mum was the P6 girls' football coach, after all.

"What? You guys are allowed to cycle to Muckleton on your own?" Erika asked with her arms folded.

Calum noticed that her American accent was becoming more Scottish.

"Course not," Leo snorted, showing off.

Calum stared at the ground.

"Well, maybe you should train for your match instead? I could get my gloves?" Erika was the star goalkeeper for the P6 girls' team.

"Can't do." Calum shrugged his shoulders at his neighbour. "We're meeting the rest of the team at the park."

"Well, *I'd* be practising if *I* were you," Erika said.

"Hey, it's not *our* fault the girls' team didn't make the playoffs." Leo grinned and picked up his BMX.

"Whatever, Leo," Erika sighed. "I hope you

guys know what you're doing. You heard what Headteacher Sanderson said."

"Come on, Cal, we're already late," Leo said.

Calum grabbed his bike and he and Leo pedalled the short distance to the park through Caleytown's sleepy Sunday morning streets.

Cat's Cradle Crew

Leo and Calum were the last to arrive. The rest of the gang looked quite small on the wide green of Caleytown's park. It was deserted.

"Where's Lewis?" Leo asked Ravi.

"He couldn't get a lift into town," Jordan replied.

"So there's only us?" Calum frowned.

"Hey, at least our star striker is here." Zack winked at Calum, who couldn't help but smile back.

"Did you bring wool?" Vik asked while typing on his phone.

Calum and Leo unzipped their bags and showed the rest of the gang. Suddenly they were all startled by a loud voice.

"Calum! Leo! What are you guys up too? Where's the football? Why aren't you playing football? Did I get the wrong day?"

They turned to see their P5 friend Fraser on his scooter.

"We're not playing football today,"
Vik answered, still looking at his phone.
"We're doing something much more
important."

"What's more important than football?"
Fraser asked, looking to Calum for support.

Calum opened his mouth to respond, just as
Vik finally looked up and burst into laughter at
Fraser's mode of transport.

"We're playing a prank at Muckleton
Primary…" he eventually explained. "But *you*
can't come, not on *that.*"

"I bet I could. The guy in the shop told my
mum it was the fastest scooter they had."

"We might need to make a quick getaway,

wee man," Zack laughed. "So it's better if you just stay behind."

Fraser looked once more at Calum.

"It's probably for the best, Frazzler," was all Calum could manage. "Don't want to get you in trouble."

"*Frazzler,*" Vik scoffed quietly at his phone screen.

Calum wasn't sure how much he liked Ravi's older brother.

"Right, Caleytown," Zack shouted. "Enough chat, let's do this!" He pulled up the hood of his red jacket and worked the pedals on his racer.

Vik took a quick selfie with his hood up and followed him.

Ravi rolled his eyes at his brother, carefully placed his hood up to the base of his quiff and pulled an impressive wheelie right across the park.

"Sorry, Fraser," Calum said before he, Jordan and Leo all followed suit. As a group, they formed a ragtag banner of hooded knights on bikes riding into battle.

Casting a glance back at Fraser, Calum saw his friend standing all alone, looking down at his scooter's small wheels.

On the old railway, leafless trees and bushes stood like skeletons along either side of the concrete path. Caught in their bones were scatterings of old crisp packets, rusting cans and sheets of newspaper.

Calum remembered cycling down this path with his dad last summer when they'd first moved to Caleytown. It had looked different then, with leaves and flowers everywhere and bees buzzing about.

Up ahead, Vik led the way with Ravi and Jordan behind. Zack was gliding along just in front of Leo and Calum.

"What would your folks do if they found out you were here?" Zack called out.

"I'd be in Major Trubs' battalion and grounded forever." Leo half-smiled as he answered.

"Me too," Calum laughed. "Especially since I told my mum I was taking her wool to go knitting at Leo's."

Leo almost lost control of his bike. "You said *what*?! Your mum will probably phone my house!"

"What was I meant to say?" said Calum, taken aback. "That I was taking the balls of wool to go and play with some kittens?!"

"I don't know! Maybe you shouldn't have got caught in the first place?"

"Don't worry, guys," Zack shouted over his shoulder. "You're with a new family now anyway – the Cat's Cradle Crew!"

Leo and Calum fell into a worried silence.

The Plan

Zack led the crew up a small slope and through a tunnel of silver birch trees. They came out at the end of a cul-de-sac lined with identical stone bungalows and parked cars. Water dripped from a recently washed red jeep but there was no one to be seen.

At the end of the street, behind a metal fence, stood the old grey-stone building of Muckleton Primary School. A playground

surrounded the building, and some sports pitches were visible further on.

Calum felt a tingle go up his spine as he looked at the pitch they'd be playing on later that week. "We should be training," he said to himself, loud enough for Leo to hear too.

His friend nodded. They were both thinking the same thing: *Is it too late to escape?!*

"Come on, Cal, Leo. Bring that wool over here," said Zack. "Cat's Cradle Crew, assemble!"

With their shoulders beginning to sag, they leaned their BMXs against the fence, ready for a quick getaway if necessary.

"Right, Jordan and Ravi: you guys are going to take the wool over to the goal and tie a

cat's cradle." Zack turned to Calum and Leo. "You two will do the same to this gate. Vik and I will stay on lookout, 'cause we're the tallest."

"That's it?" Ravi raised an eyebrow. "That's your plan?"

"Whatever, little brother," said Vikram. "Have you got a better idea?"

"Yeah, you and Zack tie the wool on the

goals yourselves!" Ravi barked.

"We're not the ones playing Muckleton, Rav," Zack said with his hands out in sympathy. "It'll mean more to your team, and you, if *you* do it."

Ravi backed down.

"I can't tie very well," Jordan muttered. He'd been unusually quiet all day.

"What?" Vik said.

"I'm not very good at knots. My mum still has to tie my shoelaces sometimes. It's why I'm wearing Velcro laces," Jordan said with reddening cheeks.

"Whatever. Don't wet your pants, McPants," Zack sighed. "Calum can do it instead. He tied

you in knots in our game of trebles so I'll bet
he can tie a good cat's cradle."

Leo cleared his throat. "If Cal's going in, then
so am I."

"Good man, Leo." Zack grinned and slapped
Leo's back. "What do you say, number nine?"

Calum didn't think he really had a choice.
He felt his head nod.

"Excellent. Let's do this thing!" Zack reached
out to shake Calum's hand. His handshake was
a lot weaker than Calum had expected.

Then Calum, Leo and Ravi each struggled
up and over the tall school gate and dropped
down on the other side.

"Hey, Ravi, this cat's cradle would keep more shots out than you!" Leo grinned, proud of the mesh of yellow-and-white wool they'd created across one set of goals.

"Maybe we *should* take up knitting,"

Calum said as he tossed a ball of wool along the goal line to Leo, a trail of yellow following in its wake like a comet. He was imagining how impressed James Cauldfield would be at their handiwork.

Ravi showed off his impressive goalkeeper reflexes to intercept the wool. "I wouldn't go that far, boys, but at least we're doing a better job than my brother and Zack." He pointed towards the gate.

Calum looked over to see Jordan trying to weave a single ball of wool through the gate's bars while Zack and Vik typed away on their phones.

"You know what? I almost feel sorry for Jordan

when I'm around your brother and Zack," Leo said.

Ravi gave him a look of mock astonishment.

"Almost," Leo said with a wink.

Calum felt a spot of rain hit his hand. It was followed by a loud clattering noise. Something felt wrong. He looked across the pitch.

The gate at the opposite end was slowly scraping open...

"OI!" Five dark shapes rushed onto the pitch. One of them was holding a football.

"It's Muckleton!" Leo shouted. "RUUUUUNNNNN!"

Heavy, cold rain began to fall as they scrambled to get away. Leo flung his rucksack on but slipped to the ground on the damp turf. Ravi grabbed him under the arms and hoisted him to his feet. They all legged it towards the gate.

Over his shoulder Calum saw the five figures coming closer. He snapped his head round just in time to see Vik and Zack grabbing their racers and speeding off towards the old railway path. Calum could hear them laughing.

"Chickens! Splitters!" Leo shouted at the older boys as they reached the gate. "Ravi, you jump over first!"

"Hurry up!" Jordan shouted. He was already

on his bike, cycling round and round in circles.

Ravi launched himself at the gate. As he lifted his leg over the top, Calum and Leo heard an awful ripping sound.

"My joggers," Ravi shouted. "They're caught!"

The sound of Muckleton's footsteps pounded closer. Calum recognised three of them: Jack Stark, Kyle Barclay and Tom Tsang, who was wearing his goalie gloves.

Leo desperately tried to free Ravi's grey tracksuit bottoms from where they'd snagged.

"What do we do?" Calum grabbed the cold bars of the gate.

"GET THEM!" Jack Stark roared.

Frazzler!

The rain hit the ground so hard it almost drowned out the sound of Muckleton's feet pounding the concrete.

"Help me!" Ravi shouted, half hanging off the gate and fully blocking Leo and Calum's escape.

Jordan stopped pedalling. He'd had an idea. "Take your trousers off!"

"What?! No way!" Ravi screamed back in disbelief.

"It's the only way, Ravi." Jordan yelled.
"IT'S THE ONLY WAY!"

Calum turned round. Jack Stark was close enough for him to make out his menacing grin.

"I see you, Cal—"

Crrrreeaaaakkkkk!

The gate clicked open, with Ravi still attached to it.

"Come on!" a familiar voice yelped. Fraser's bright blue eyes shone through the downpour. "Why's Ravi on top of the gate? Why didn't you just open it?"

"Frazzler! Man, are we glad to see you!"
Leo shouted.

The gate swung a full arc to bang off its
hinges, sending their goalkeeper on a dive he
didn't want to make. He landed on his hands.

"Argh! MY FINGERS!" Ravi looked a sorry
sight sprawled on the wet pavement in ripped
jogging bottoms. He cradled his left hand in his
right.

"Run, Ravi, run!" Leo shouted. He grabbed Ravi by his right arm and hauled him to his feet.

They stumbled to their bikes while Fraser closed the gate to buy them some time. Then he jumped on his scooter, pushed himself forward and crouched to make himself more aerodynamic.

Crrrreeeaaaakkkkk!

The gate swung open again behind them.

Calum looked over his shoulder, expecting to see their rivals in pursuit, but they'd stopped behind Jack Stark's pale, outstretched arms.

Muckleton's captain was saying something he couldn't hear.

"Come on, Cal!" Leo shouted. "Keep pedalling!"

The lads shot down the cul-de-sac like it was the final stretch in the Tour de France. A spray of water came off their back tyres, creating a fine mist that looked like exhaust smoke. Fraser did well to keep up on his scooter.

"Where are Zack and Vik?" Calum yelled at Jordan. The rain had eased off to a drizzle but his wet, straw-like hair kept scratching his eyes.

"Who knows?!" Jordan shouted over his shoulder before hurtling down to the railway path through the corridor of birch trees. "Vik took a selfie, then they bolted."

"Some friends," Leo said as they reached the safety of the path itself. "You ok, Ravi?"

Ravi didn't answer. He looked pale, and grimaced every time his bike hit a bump. He could only hold his left handlebar with his pinkie. His injured fingers pointed forward. They looked swollen.

"Do you think the prank will work?" Calum felt his adrenaline wearing off. "Did we get under Muckleton's skin?"

No one answered. Caleytown's players cycled back to their home town in silence.

Calum locked his bike up round the back of his house and entered the kitchen. He heard his parents switch the television off. That wasn't a good sign.

His mum appeared at the door to the dining room, switched the light on and looked at the rain dripping off her son onto the kitchen floor.

"You'd better give me what you've knitted before it shrinks," she said.

Leighton appeared behind her, took one look at Calum and trotted back to his warm bed with his tail down.

"It's fine, I... left it at Leo's." Calum stumbled through his words.

"That's funny," his mum said, "because I called Leo's mum, and she told me you weren't, in fact, knitting. She said you and Leo had gone for a cycle. Nice day for it, I guess."

79

Calum's dad appeared behind his mum in the doorway. He didn't look impressed either. They stared at him, waiting for an explanation.

The only noise was the ticking of the kitchen clock and the dripping of Calum's wet clothes on the floor.

A Special
Team Meeting

"I'm grounded for a week, with no internet –
meaning no Scotland Stars," said Leo. "Plus,
thanks to Calum, the Master of Deception, I now
have to learn how to knit – with my mum."

"Ha ha ha! Can you make
me a woolly hat to
wear for training?"
Erika asked. She
and Sally were
loving every detail

of the boys' punishment, as they made their way to school on Monday morning.

"How about you, Cal?" Sally asked.

"Same," Calum sulked. "I told my folks that we'd cycled to Muckleton with Ravi's older brother to check out their pitch. They didn't care that an older boy was there. They were really, *really* angry that I'd lied."

"How did you explain the wool?" Leo asked.

"I said everyone at school is mad into cat's cradle. She didn't buy it."

Sally hooted with laughter.

Erika was shaking her head. "Why on earth did you think tying wool all over Muckleton's goals was a good idea? Who *does* that? I mean,

is it a *Scottish* thing?"

"I'm not arguing." Leo sniffed, then sneezed his way through the school gates.

Sally gave him serious side-eye. "I'm going to run ahead of you knitters before Leo gives me the plague. C'mon, Erika."

Why didn't we just play football? Calum thought to himself for the twentieth time as he watched the girls scamper away.

"Ha-CHOO!" Leo sneezed, again.

"Just a quick message for the boys' football team." Mr McKlop's voice echoed in the gymnastics hall at the start of P.E. "There's to be

a special team meeting before practice tonight. Come here before you get changed. And don't be late."

Calum felt his stomach fall into his socks. A special team meeting could only mean one thing.

"You don't think Sanderson found out, do you?" he whispered to Leo in the queue for the gym horse.

Leo shrugged. He was unusually quiet but, then again, his nose was so blocked he had to breathe through his mouth.

When it was Calum's turn, he took a giant run-up to the springboard. But with a head full of potential playoff disasters, he sprung way

too hard, flipped head-over-heels above the horse and landed flat on his back on the crash mat.

"Calum... CALUM, are you alright?" Mr McKlop came running over, his whistle bouncing around his neck.

Calum could hear Sally hooting with laughter – she wasn't the only one. He sat up.

"Ok, you're ok," Mr McKlop said to himself. "Just to emphasise, class. You're to leapfrog the

obstacle, not front-flip over it like Mr Ferguson here."

Calum looked across at his classmates and saw that Jordan and Leo were the only ones not laughing. After Mr McKlop's announcement, they both looked like prisoners awaiting trial.

Hours later, Jordan, Leo and Calum were still wearing the same expressions in the players' meeting. Ravi was absent.

The team sat in silence until Mr McKlop strode into the hall with Erika in tow.

Calum's teacher took his glasses off, breathed on them and rubbed them clean with

his corduroy jacket. Calum tried to catch Erika's eye, but couldn't. *What's she doing here?* he thought. *Has she told on us?!*

"Gentlemen, and lady, I have some good news and some bad news." Mr McKlop looked at his squad.

Three of his players didn't look back at him.

"The bad news is that Mrs Gupta called today to let me know that Ravi fell off his bike at the weekend, and fractured a finger."

Lewis and Jordan exchanged a glance.

"It's really unfortunate to lose such a key member of the team, especially as we have no reserve goalkeeper." Mr McKlop looked at Erika. "But after chatting to Coach Brown, and checking

the Scotland Stars tournament rules, I'm pleased to announce that Erika has agreed to play for us in goal against Muckleton. She's a very talented keeper and we're lucky to have her."

Janek nodded and started to clap. A few of the players' mouths fell open, and words fell out of Jordan's. "But she's... she's... a girl."

"And you'll be an unused substitute, Mr McPride, with any more of that chat. Am I clear?"

Jordan nodded in slow motion.

Flooded with relief, Calum grinned at Erika. He had no qualms about her playing: she saved most of his shots in his back garden after all.

"Great, now get changed for practice! We've got a playoff to get ready for!"

"Why didn't Muckleton tell on us?" Jordan whispered as they made their way out of the hall.

"No idea," Calum said.

"They're up to something." Jordan nodded thoughtfully. "Jack Stark will have a plan. You just watch."

Leo sneezed.

The Shadows

This hotly anticipated first playoff between favourites Muckleton and Central Wildcats' plucky underdogs Caleytown really will be 'A Tale of Two Goalkeepers'.

Calum's mum arrived at their computer desk with two mugs of hot chocolate. Even though Calum was still grounded, Erika was allowed round because her parents were out on their 'date night'.

News of her inclusion in the Caleytown team had spread like wildfire. Scotland Stars reporter Reiss Robertson had even visited the school to do a feature on her, and they were watching it now.

In the black-and-white corner we have Tom Tsang. Since he arrived at Muckleton mid-season, Tsang has been attracting interest from scouts with some miraculous saves.

"Weird," said Erika. "Ooh, here's my bit!"

"Wow, I look good," said Erika. "I hope King's Park's scouts don't clock your terrible shooting ability though, Cal."

93

"Yeah, maybe," Calum said, absently.

"Only joking, Cal! C'mon, aren't you excited about the playoffs?" Erika said, her bushy ponytail bobbing about on her back. "I can't wait!"

"Course. I'm just worried about the pranks Muckleton are planning for revenge."

"What?! The Calum I know would usually be too busy worrying about the football to care about that other stuff."

Erika blew on her hot chocolate and took a big gulp. Calum hadn't even touched his.

Before they knew it, the Caleytown P6 team were arriving at Muckleton Primary in their minibus.

Calum, Leo and Jordan exchanged nervous glances as the school gates came into view.

"Welcome to Muckleton!" Muckleton's coach greeted the Caleytown squad in the damp car park. He had a square jaw and a shaved head. "My players have insisted on carrying your kit bag for you. It's unusual for them to be so courteous."

A few Muckleton players, including Jack Stark, scuttled out of the shadows in their black blazers to grab the big bag containing Caleytown's strips, footballs and jackets for subs.

"Much appreciated." Mr McKlop winced as Muckleton's coach crushed his hand in a handshake. "Are you watching this, Caleytown? You might learn something."

"We're watching them, alright," Jordan mumbled. Calum and Erika followed him off the bus and through to the changing rooms.

"Go, Erika, go! Woohoo!" a couple of girls in Muckleton uniforms shouted when they saw Caleytown's new goalkeeper walking down the

corridor. They'd obviously seen the Scotland Stars report too.

Erika waved. "Hey guys!"

The old, draughty school was like something out of a ghost story. The team got changed in double-quick time so they could get back outside. Even Jordan got ready quickly: he pulled on his thermal top, thermal leggings, special sock tape and, for the first time, a sweatband on his head.

Leo couldn't help himself when he saw it. "Jordan, since when did you need a sweatband? You haven't got long hair, and it's freezing outside."

"In case it rains like it did on Sunday," Jordan

said warily. "My mum says it will keep my hair gel out of my eyes."

"So would not wearing gel in the first place... ha-CHOO!"

Leo sneezed. He still wasn't well following the downpour.

When they emerged from the changing rooms, the wood smoke from the houses nearby had created a haze on the pitch. Strangely, for a playoff, there was hardly anyone there to watch. It made Caleytown's home matches look like carnivals.

Calum studied the goal they'd pranked just a few days before. Only one strand of their cat's cradle was left, tied to a post as if Muckleton had left it as a reminder.

Mr McKlop watched his team's tentative approach with a smile. "Here we are, Caleytown, playoff time. In my opinion, we can't lose today, because we've already won by making it this far. So don't look so worried, guys."

The boys stared at their kitbag, desperate to put their strips on over their t-shirts for the extra warmth.

"Here we go. Today's team is as follows..."

TEAM FORMATION:

Erika (goal keeper)

Jordan (defence)　　　**Janek** (defence, C)

Fraser (right wing)　　**Lewis** (midfield)　　**Leo** (left wing)

Calum (striker)

SUBS: RYAN, MAX, EWAN

It was an attacking line-up. If Calum hadn't been so wary of potential Muckleton pranks, he would have been delighted. But pulling on his yellow jersey helped to ease some of his worries.

Still, he could feel Jack Stark grinning at him. And that's when the itching started.

The First-Leg Itch

Distracted by an insane need to scratch,
Caleytown could do nothing to stop
Muckleton running through them and scoring,
straight from kick off. With three players
bearing down on her, Erika didn't stand
a chance.

"Come on, Caleytown,"
Mr McKlop shouted from the
sideline. "What's got into you?"

Calum scratched at his itchy

chest, waiting to restart the match, but that only spread the itchiness to his shoulders.

It felt like a cloud of midges had got under his top.

He turned to face his teammates.

Jordan was squirming like he had spiders under his thermals.

Janek was slapping at his arms and banging his chest as if trying to kill the itching stone dead.

Leo was scratching and sneezing at the same time.

Fraser was running back and forward yelping like a dog being bitten by fleas.

On the sideline, three Caleytown subs wriggled and jiggled like they were at a disco.

Mr McKlop watched helplessly from the sideline.

Leo kicked off to Calum, but he couldn't focus and practically gave the ball away.

"What's wrong?" Jack Stark said as Calum tried to tackle the ball back from him. "Are your strips made of *wool*, or something?"

"You've put itching powder in our strips!" Calum hissed at Stark.

"Get the ball back, Calum!" Lewis despaired. His face had gone beetroot from the unbearable need to scratch.

Jack Stark laughed and sprinted away. Leo tried to track him but a huge sneeze – followed by a scratching fit – stopped him in his tracks.

Why did we do that stupid prank? Calum thought again, his fingers buried in an itchy armpit.

The Muckleton midfielder moved effortlessly forward, prompting Kyle Barclay to start moving through the gears.

"My man," Janek said, his voice unusually strained. His new tactic was to ignore the fiery itching under his top.

In goal, Erika was fine, if a little confused.

She'd brought her very own goalkeeper top and was therefore itch-free. She bounced on her toes as Jack Stark curled a hanging cross into the box.

On the penalty spot, Kyle Barclay tussled with Janek to get to the ball. He had the height advantage, and leapt to power a header at goal.

"Ugh!" Erika threw herself down to her left and palmed the ball onto the post. It rebounded out towards Jack Stark.

In a flash, the dark-haired midfielder was onto the rebound.

Erika pushed herself to her feet.

"Jack's ball," Muckleton's captain shouted before smacking the rebound, first time.

"Ooft!" Erika winced as Stark's shot pushed the air from her chest. She fell back, the ball nestled in her midriff.

"What a save!" Calum shouted, punching the air before resuming his two-handed scratching.

"Awesome, Erika! You're awesome, Erika!" Fraser shouted from the ground. He had dropped onto the turf and was moving along the ground like a slug to quell the itching.

Winded, Erika hadn't got up yet. The ref blew his whistle and Mr McKlop ran to check she was ok. He was carrying a sponge and a dozen water bottles.

Lewis, who looked like he was doing a strange dance, saw the water bottles and sprinted straight for their coach.

Fraser flipped himself onto his feet and made a beeline for the bottles too.

Calum watched as they each grabbed a bottle, unscrewed the caps and doused themselves in water. Sweet relief spread over their faces.

"Guys, GUYS!"

"It works! IT WORKS!"

Seven more players ran at Mr McKlop, itching and scratching. One by one they poured water over their heads and started a chorus of *Ahhhhh*s.

Erika slowly stood up – more to get out of the way of her dripping teammates than anything else.

"Are you ok, Erika?" Mr McKlop asked with concern. "That was a wonder save, by the way."

"Yes sir, thanks sir," Erika panted. "Just a little winded is all. It'll pass."

Caleytown's coach turned to face his nine soggy players.

"Guys... I can only apologise," he said, pulling his hair back with both hands. "I'd better look into buying different detergent."

Out the corner of his eye, Calum saw Jack Stark high-five one of his teammates.

"Yes!" said a soaking Jordan. "The headband kept the gel out of my eyes."

Leo's laugh turned into a sneezing fit.

NATIONAL SOCCER SEVENS TOURNAMENT
CENTRAL WILDCATS LEAGUE
MUCKLETON 1 – 0 CALEYTOWN

Only heroics from Caleytown keeper Erika Brown stopped this two-legged playoff tie from being over in the first half. Unfortunately for Caleytown, even she couldn't stop Muckleton's Jack Stark from walking in the only goal of the match in the first minute. Then again, her teammates didn't do much to help her during a truly bizarre start to this match. Up the other end, the highly-rated Tommy Tsang actually could've taken his gloves *off* for once.

Caleytown's attack was blunt in the first half and not much better in the second when tricky winger Leo Nkwanu sneezed his way to the substitutes' bench.

Thanks to Erika Brown, and a captain's performance from Janek Powolski in defence, everything is still in the balance ahead of the second leg in Caleytown next week. Both sets of players will be *itching* to put in a good performance in that match, as there are rumours circulating that some King's Park Athletic scouts will be there to watch.

Now for the Next Trick

To get in the zone for the second leg, Caleytown's P6 players once again met in the park for a Saturday kickabout. Calum and Leo's groundings were over, so they went along with Erika and Fraser, with Leighton in tow.

"How are you feeling, Leo?" Erika asked. Like Tsang, she already had her goalie gloves on.

"Better," Leo said. "But I think the ultimate cure will be beating Muckleton in the second leg."

"Too right!" Calum and Fraser agreed.

"Can I hear clapping?" Leo said as they arrived at the park.

"Erika, Erika, Erika!" Jordan and Lewis led the chant. Erika blushed and made her way over to where they were standing. The whole team was there.

"You guys are the best!" She was beaming. "But I'm sure Ravi would have been as good."

Ravi smiled, but he still looked gutted about missing the games.

Erika tightened her glove straps. "What're we playing then, boys?"

"Six versus five," Janek said, taking control. "Ravi is going to go in goals but can't use his hands, so his team gets six."

"Sounds fair!" said Leo, grabbing the ball and taking it for a dribble.

Calum was on Ravi's team and Leo was on Erika's, so the two best friends soon found themselves tussling over the ball. Both giggled as they barged into each other.

Calum, with his extra weight, won the bout and dribbled forward.

Jordan came out to meet him, side on.

Full of confidence, Calum tried a 'roulette' – a move his dad had shown him online while he'd been grounded. It was something one of his dad's favourite players, Zinedine Zidane, had made famous. Calum had been practising it in the garden ever since.

In one movement, he pushed off his left foot and dragged the ball back with his right. Launching his body into a 360-degree spin, he turned his back to Jordan, caught the ball under his left studs, and pulled it round into the space behind him.

Roulette

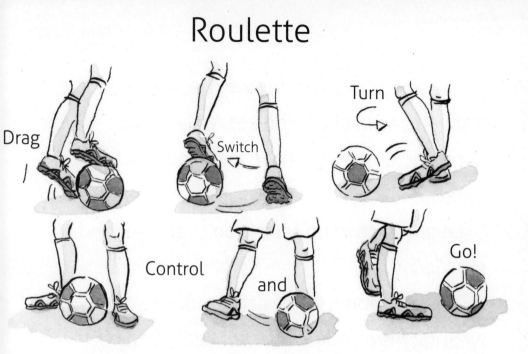

Drag

Switch

Turn

Control

and

Go!

To Calum's astonishment, it worked!

Erika ran out to dive at his feet but he curled the ball around her and into the goal.

Leighton ran to stop the ball.

"That went over the post," Jordan said.

"Yeah, right!" Calum was already trying to place the goal in his top ten of the best goals he'd ever scored.

"You have to give him that goal, McPants." With a screech of bike brakes, Vik and Zack appeared on their racers in the middle of the pitch.

Leighton gave up on the ball, ran over and growled.

"Gather round, lads," Zack said. He was wearing his trendy red jacket again and his hair was freshly cut.

Janek sucked his teeth but everyone else complied.

"I hear that you're a better goalie than my brother," Vik said to Erika.

Ravi rolled his eyes.

"And who are you?" Erika raised an eyebrow.

"Whoa there, girl! We come in peace," Zack laughed.

Erika crossed her arms and stared at him.

"So I heard about the itching powder," Zack said, ignoring her. "How are we going to get back at Mucklebum?"

Zack's question was met by silence. The way he'd spoken to Erika was the final straw for Calum. He took a deep breath and planted both his feet on the ground.

"*We* are going to get our own back by beating Muckleton in the second leg."

Yeah!

Proper football.

Too right!

Zack jerked his head away like a boxer avoiding a punch. "Whoa! There's fat chance of that happening, Cal, unless you get under their skin with a good prank," he laughed.

Ravi looked at his broken fingers and clenched his other hand into a fist. "Like you guys, do you mean?"

"Chill out, Ravs," Vikram scoffed.

Ravi's quiff mirrored the hackles that were up on Leighton's back.

"What you conveniently forgot to mention is that you *lost!*" Ravi shouted this last word at his brother and Zack.

A few of the parents looked over from the play-park.

"Despite all your 'great pranks', you LOST your playoff against Muckleton in P6 – *and again in P7!*"

"Whatever, Ravi. I think you need to calm down, mate," Zack said, his eyes suddenly less friendly.

"He's not *your* mate, *mate*. He's *my* mate." Jordan flipped his collar up and stood next to Ravi. "Now, if you don't mind, we've got a playoff to get ready for."

Erika let out a delighted squeal.

For a moment, nobody spoke. Calum was worried about what might happen next.

"Come on, let's get out of here," said Vikram, to everyone's relief. "It's boring hanging around with P6 babies anyway."

Zack grabbed Jordan's football and hoofed it halfway across the park. "Very mature, Zachary," said Erika.

Zack and Vik got on their racers and rode off into town.

"Do I get that goal then?" Calum asked with a grin on his face.

Jordan glared at Calum for a second before a big smile spread over his face. "Go on then... Even though it was a lucky spin..."

The Double Bluff

Under Mr McKlop's instruction, Calum stood in Caleytown Primary's sunny car park to welcome Muckleton to their school.

"Are your parents coming to watch?" Calum asked both Leo and Fraser.

"Yup, my dad's getting off work early to come," said Leo.

They both looked along the line to Fraser.

"Just my mum. My dad lives in England now," he said.

Calum opened his mouth to speak, but Muckleton's bus rolled into the car park and came to a quick stop. The Muckleton players dropped down onto the tarmac in their black blazers like soldiers out of a helicopter.

"Weirdos. What do they think we're going to do?" Leo whispered in Calum's ear.

Mr McKlop shook the other coach's massive hand again, while Fraser stood smiling at the Muckleton players. Only Kyle Barclay smiled back – he was too big to be scared of anything.

"We can carry our own kitbag, sir," Jack Stark said to his coach when Leo offered to take it.

"For goodness' sake, Jack! Be polite," his square-headed coach barked back. "Here... Leo, isn't it? Could you fill our water bottles please?"

Jack Stark stared at the bottles as if he was memorising how they looked.

Nerves settled on Caleytown's changing room like a blanket. Everyone sat in silence waiting

for Jordan to finish getting ready. He'd put on his thermal trousers and polo neck. Next, he inserted a chip into his top that his dad could track on an app. Then, finally, he pulled on his last item of sportswear: the headband.

Leo looked at the headband and bit his lip. He let it pass without comment. Jordan nodded at Janek and the captain led the team out.

Outside, the sun was shining and the Astroturf gleamed like a new toy. The players' parents and friends cheered the team onto the pitch. A few of the other P6s had even made a banner that read:

**WE BELIEVE
IN CALEYTOWN F.C.!**

"This. Is. Amazing," said Leo.

The shopkeeper, Mr Aziz, waved from the sideline next to Calum's parents, who'd invited him along. He'd never been to one of their matches before.

Scanning the crowd, Calum felt his nerves crackle as he spotted Old Bill, the King's Park Athletic scout, standing with his small notepad and pen.

Muckleton ran out next in their black-and-white stripes, looking as big as they always did. The handful of Muckleton parents who'd made the journey clapped. Jack Stark immediately went to check their water bottles.

"Maybe no prank is the best prank we could pull," Calum thought out loud.

"Yeah, it's called a double bluff," said Erika, slamming her gloved hands together and smiling.

"Same team as the first leg, gentlemen," Mr McKlop said. "Now, go out and enjoy yourselves!"

The players gingerly pulled their strips on, glad there would be no itching this time.

The referee called the two captains to the centre spot.

Calum saw the coin glint as it spun in the air between Janek and Jack Stark. It landed on the pitch. The ref pointed at Janek, who motioned to change ends. It was a good call: the sun would be at Caleytown's backs and shine in Muckleton's eyes.

Calum and Erika passed Jack Stark as they jogged to the other half of the pitch.

"Why are we changing ends, Ferguson?" Stark's frown formed fault lines on his face. "What have you two done to the goal?"

Calum shrugged.

Erika shook her head. "That guy has got some serious trust issues."

A hush fell over the crowd as Kyle Barclay

and a floppy-haired teammate stood over the ball to kick off. Out on the wings, Leo and Fraser looked like racing cars waiting for the lights to go green.

The referee's whistle drew a huge cheer from the crowd, and Calum ran straight for Kyle Barclay. The big striker did his best to protect the ball, but he was in unfamiliar territory.

Lewis dived in from the other side and stole possession.

Out wide, Leo screamed for a pass. Lewis pinged it out to him and kept running.

To the delight of the home support, Leo danced down the wing and passed to Calum.

"That's my boy!" Leo's dad shouted.

"Where have you set off the stinkbombs?" Jack Stark hissed as Calum controlled Leo's pass.

Calum ignored him and waited for Stark to lunge in before doing a perfect roulette past him.

The crowd roared.

"Watch out, Tom!" Stark shouted to his keeper. "There might be stinkbombs on the ground."

Tom Tsang looked at the ground, but he should have been looking at Leo, who was ghosting in at the near post.

Calum pretended to shoot but, instead, rolled the ball into his friend's path.

With Tsang well and truly confused, Leo squeezed the ball into the bottom corner.

YYYYYYYYYYYYESSSSSSSSSSSS S S SS!

Caleytown's players swarmed round Leo.
Even Ravi ran onto the pitch, holding his
injured fingers in the air like a foam hand.

The ref blew his whistle at him. "Off the
pitch, laddy."

Calum couldn't believe they'd already cancelled out Muckleton's goal from the first leg. It was 1–1 on aggregate.

"That was *your* fault, Jack!" Tom Tsang said. "Quit acting crazy. Can we start playing actual football now?!"

"Alright, Tsang. Keep your gloves on," Jack huffed.

"I always do, Jack," Tom Tsang answered.

The Unexpected

Minutes before half-time, Calum sidestepped Muckleton's last defender and wrapped his yellow boot around the ball, to send it spinning towards the top corner of Tsang's goal. He could feel his arms beginning to rise in celebration, when Tsang flew like a fighter jet to pluck his shot out of the air.

"Yeeaa... OHHH!" Calum shouted. It wasn't the first of his attempts that Tsang had saved.

The keeper launched a Muckleton counter-attack

with a monster throw. Kyle Barclay bounced off Jordan, then Lewis, before firing a bending shot at Erika's goal.

Like a fielder in baseball, Erika watched it weave through the air towards her. At the last moment, her hand shot up to parry it over the crossbar.

"Way to go, Erika!" Coach Brown, Erika's mum, bounced up and down on the sideline with Calum's mum and Sally.

The resulting corner led to a meaty header from Jordan. The ball landed kindly for Leo, who pounced like a lion onto its prey. He tore back up the pitch.

"Leo! LEO!" Calum shouted.

Leo thumped a curling cross his way.

It was perfect.

The crowd disappeared from Calum's view – it was just him and the ball, which was still hanging in the air. He threw himself at it and powered a header down to Tsang's right.

Tsang reacted so quickly, it seemed to take the rest of his body a moment to catch up with his arm. He hung motionless for a second, his feet higher than his head, and clawed Calum's header to the side of the goal.

There was an "Oooo" from both sides of the pitch. Even though Calum hadn't put Caleytown ahead, the crowd knew they'd seen something special. Up the other end of the pitch, Erika sportingly applauded the save.

The first half had been so end-to-end, the ref was worn out. He didn't even have the puff to blow his whistle. Instead he huffed, "That's half-time, lads."

Caleytown's players gulped air and water on the sideline. Mr McKlop looked at his team, the sun reflecting off his thick-rimmed specs. He'd tied his tracksuit top around his waist.

"Honestly, gentlemen, I couldn't be prouder of you today." He glanced down the sideline and smiled at a pregnant woman sitting on a chair. She had long, curly black hair and a kind face. It didn't take a genius to work out it was *Mrs* McKlop. "Ewan, on you go for Lewis; Ryan, you're on for Fraser. I'll keep making subs to give everyone a chance to play. Other than that, just keep doing what you're doing."

Let's go, Caley, let's go!

Come on, Caleytown!

'Mon the geese!

The crowd cheered Caleytown back onto the pitch. Calum ran to catch up with Erika.

"Can you give me any tips? How can I beat Spiderman in goals?" he quizzed his friend. "I feel like I'm never going to score."

"The unexpected," Erika said without hesitation.

"What?"

"Do something unexpected. Trust me."
Erika looked Calum in the eye. "Keepers *hate* the unexpected."

"The unexpected?" Calum's head spun. "How can I *plan* to do something unexpected?"

"You'll figure it out, Cal," Erika said, pulling on a baseball cap to protect her eyes against the sun. She threaded her bushy ponytail out the back. "Now, if you'll excuse me, I've got a goal to guard."

"The unexpected," Calum whispered to himself, as he and Erika ran in opposite directions.

Who'll Blink First?

As the second half wore on, a few clouds drifted in front of the sun, causing the temperature to drop. The crowd zipped up their jackets and hugged themselves tightly.

If the first half had been an end-to-end battle, the second half was a case of who would blink first. If neither team lost concentration, they would be heading for a shoot-out.

"I hope you've been brushing up on your penalties," Jack Stark said with a sneer.

"We've been meeting up every day after school to practise them."

Calum did his best to ignore Stark, but his words left him anxious. Caleytown rarely practised penalties – it wasn't Mr McKlop's style.

To make matters worse, Vik and Zack had arrived on the sideline – Muckleton's sideline. They were there in time to see Calum attempt a back-heel at goal, when he would normally have spun and shot. He'd caught Tsang off guard... but Muckleton's keeper had still saved it.

Tsang booted the ball away, but Ewan intercepted it in midfield.

"Ewan! EWAN!" Calum's hand shot up for a through pass.

Ewan managed to pelt the ball back up to Calum before being buffeted over by Kyle Barclay.

Calum took the ball in his stride and saw that Tsang was standing just off his line. He got close enough to shoot and, this time, he went for a crazy lob.

Tom Tsang scrambled back, racing the football to his goals. He flung himself towards the net and somehow caught the ball. Not only that, he landed holding the ball just in front of his line.

"Unlucky again, number nine! Great effort," Mr Aziz shouted.

Calum turned to see his friend's bushy

moustache curved in a smile.

Over on the other sideline, he heard Zack shouting, "Stop showing off. Just put the ball in the net!"

Calum blocked out the older boy's 'advice'. He knew Erika was right: he'd almost beaten Tom Tsang by doing something unexpected, twice.

Now it was Muckleton's turn to break forward. Their floppy-haired, skilful midfielder drifted across Caleytown's box, bringing Janek and Jordan with him.

"Back-heel!" Stark screamed.

The languid midfielder answered the call by setting Stark up nicely.

Ewan ran across to block and Erika stayed on her toes.

Muckleton's captain shot, but Ewan thrust his boot in the way to deflect the ball.

Wrong-footed, Erika's momentum was taking her away from the deflected strike. The goal gaped open like a baseball catcher's mitt.

In the foreground, Calum saw Stark's hands lift into the air for the celebration. But Erika arched her back like a cat to form a flying U shape...

Caleytown's keeper somehow managed to tip the ball onto the crossbar and out for a corner with the toe of her right boot!

Stark's hands fell to his face. "Aw, come on!"

The crowd cheered with relief.

"They can't beat you, Erika Brown!" Sally hollered. "They don't know how!"

Erika's mum came in for a high-five.

After a goal-mouth scramble from the resulting corner, Jordan came away with the ball and looked downfield. He tried to find Calum with a pass, but hoofed it out of play.

"Nice pass, Sweatband McPants," Calum heard Vik scoff as Muckleton's coach retrieved the ball.

Jordan heard it too. He pulled his sweatband off and threw if over the sideline.

"Oooo…" Vik and Zack teased Jordan. "Jordi's having a tantrum."

"Shut up, Vik!" Ravi yelled across the pitch.

"Come on, guys, forget about those idiots, let's get this winner," Leo shouted, before turning to Calum. "I don't fancy taking a penalty against Tom Tsang. Do you?"

Calum shook his head and watched Muckleton's winger throw the ball in to Kyle Barclay.

To everyone's surprise, Jordan slid in, won the ball cleanly and got to his feet in one movement.

On the sideline, Vik's mouth hung half-open, ready to shout something, but nothing came out.

Jordan bore forward. His face was pure concentration.

But the rest of Caleytown's faces expressed pure panic – they all knew that dribbling wasn't Jordan's strong point.

Somehow he held off a challenge from Jack

Stark, and kept the ball at his feet. He looked down the pitch, swung his leg like a cricket bat and curled an unusually accurate pass out towards Leo on the wing.

Everyone breathed a sigh of relief.

Leo controlled the ball and jinked to the sideline to shake off his marker. He drew his leg back and smashed a low cross towards Calum in the box.

Calum's marker let out a rattly grunt, stuck a foot out and skewed the ball up, up, and up...

Calum saw the ball hanging like a full moon in the sky.

He saw the King's Park scout standing over by the corner flag.

He saw his mum and dad on the sideline
with Mr Aziz and little Leighton. And he heard
Erika's advice in his ears before he saw his own
foot fly up over his head to smash the hanging
football back down to earth.

Tom Tsang stood rooted to the spot.
He could only watch as Calum's overhead kick
sailed past him and into the net.

Calum lay on his back as the clouds parted.
He felt the sun hit his face.

16
Heroes Glen

YYYYYYYeeeeeeeeeEEEEEESSSSSSSSSSSS!

The roar of the crowd was louder than Calum had ever heard before. He jumped up from the ground and didn't quite know where to run. It didn't matter. All his teammates were running towards him anyway. Muckleton were on their knees.

"What was that?!" Leo shouted in Calum's ear.

"The unexpected." Calum winked at Erika,

who'd joined the mob of Caleytown players swarming around him.

But the game wasn't over yet. Muckleton still had two minutes to equalise.

Jack Stark rushed past them all. He grabbed the ball out of the net and carried it back to the halfway line.

Caleytown's players dispersed like yellow confetti for the restart.

"Look." Leo pointed over at Muckleton's sideline as he passed Calum.

Zack and Vik were pushing their bikes to the exit.

"Goodbye to bad news," said Calum.

"Too right."

As the ref restarted the game, Jack Stark ran forward. He found his floppy-haired teammate, who hit a first-time pass to Kyle Barclay.

The sun was back out now. Erika shuffled her baseball cap low over her eyes and watched Muckleton's athletic striker like a hawk.

He powered forward and shot. Still buzzing after Calum's overhead kick, the crowd watched Barclay's attempt flying towards goal...

PPFt!

...and stop in Erika's gloves. She held on to it for a second or two, frozen in silence. Then the referee blew his whistle for full-time.

The next thing Caleytown knew, they were surrounded by their classmates, who'd invaded the pitch.

Sally sprinted over to Erika and launched herself at her friend, knocking her baseball cap off her head. "You were amazing, Erika!"

"Thanks." Calum heard Erika laugh, her cap hanging off her ponytail. On the halfway line, he was surrounded by excited voices.

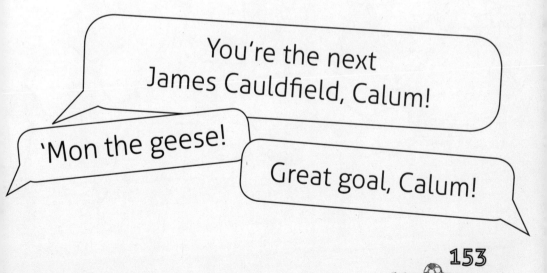

You're the next James Cauldfield, Calum!

'Mon the geese!

Great goal, Calum!

Up the other end of the pitch, Muckleton's coach was trying to comfort his players. They lay around on the ground in their black-and-white strips.

Mr McKlop and Janek gathered the team and told them to go and shake their opponents' hands.

Calum jogged over to Jack Stark first and offered his hand.

"No pranks then?" Stark asked, hauling himself to his feet.

"Not today. We just wanted to play football."

"Good idea. Best not to waste any more wool."

Calum laughed. "Or itching powder."

"Aye." Jack tried to laugh. "You'll be representing the Central Wildcats at Heroes Glen now. Don't let us down."

Calum shook hands with Muckleton's captain. and walked over to where his teammates were gathering around Mr McKlop. Sometime during the celebrations, Mr McKlop had lost his glasses. Calum couldn't remember seeing their coach without them before.

"Incredible, guys!" Mr McKlop said, squinting at his players. "Our next stop is the national final at Heroes Glen Indoor Arena! You lot up for it?" The team cheered.

"But first, please help me find my glasses..."

"That was some goal, Cal." Calum's dad smiled at him as they set off home with Leo's family. "How are you guys feeling about the grand finale?"

"Piece of cake, Mr Ferguson." Leo grinned. "No one can stop the geese now!"

Calum's dad laughed and shook his head. Mr Nkwanu ruffled Leo's hair.

"Now, Cal, Leo, don't get your hopes up, but we've chatted to Old Bill, the scout," Calum's mum joined in.

Calum's hopes soared – he couldn't help it.

"He's going to come to the finals and bring King's Park's head of scouting with him. They want to watch you both."

Even though they'd just won, Calum could feel a new kind of pressure building in his chest. His mum put a hand on his cheek.

"Don't worry so much, love. I'm sure he'll be impressed with what he sees."

"Yeah, Cal, and if not, maybe we could knit him something special," Leo whispered.

DANNY SCOTT, a die-hard football fan, works for Scottish Book Trust and is the goalie for Scotland Writers F.C.

ALICE A. MORENTORN is a children's book illustrator and a teacher at Emile Cohl School of Arts in Lyon, France.

NATIONAL SOCCER SEVENS TOURNAMENT
CENTRAL WILDCATS LEAGUE
CALEYTOWN 2 – 0 MUCKLETON

Caleytown Primary were a different team in this second leg of playoffs against Muckleton Primary this week. It wasn't just confident keeper Tom Tsang standing open-mouthed after a nifty goal from winger Leo Nkwanu in the first seconds of play.

Muckleton fought back after their initial shock, wowing the crowd with some athletic saves from Tsang and powerful shots at Caleytown's stand-in keeper Erika Brown. Members of the crowd were fortunate so see some real creativity on both sides as keepers and strikers were put to the test again and again. It looked like the game would head to penalties as both sides remained 1–1 on aggregate... until Caleytown's Calum Ferguson scored the deciding goal with a beautiful overhead kick.

Against all odds, newly formed team Caleytown Primary have fought their way up the Central Wildcats league to play at the Scotland Stars National Soccer Sevens Tournament. We're excited to see how they will hold up against the rest of the nation's best.

RUMOURS

⚽ Royal Road Primary of the Glasgow Steelers league became the first team in Scotland to book their places at Scotland Stars F.C.'s National Finals. Rumours are flying that Royal Road's P6s, funded by billionaire Proctor Hampton, might just be the best primary school team in Scotland.

⚽ We've heard whispers that scouts and reps from professional teams all over the UK will be present at the Scotland Stars National Soccer Sevens Tournament. Join us as we spot famous faces and cover the action at Heroes Glen on the day!

Email: fitba@scotlandstarsfc.co.uk for your thoughts on the action.

Mr McKlop's coaching corner!

Do you want to learn the roulette move made famous by Zinedine Zidane, Diego Maradona and Calum Ferguson? Done well, the roulette is a beautiful way to change direction and roll round defenders without ever losing control of the ball.

⚽ The Roulette ⚽

Remember, you don't need to be able to perform new moves at full speed. Practise these steps at a walk first, then gradually build up the pace.

1. Place a ball a couple of paces away from a cone, or a friend.
2. Walk, jog or run up to the ball and drag it back with your right foot.
3. Now plant the same foot where the ball was and begin to turn back on yourself, anti-clockwise.
4. Catch the rolling ball under your left boot and drag it with you as you complete your turn past your cone (or opponent).
5. Now practise the same move with your other foot.
6. Do it faster, then do it with a rolling ball instead of a stationary one.

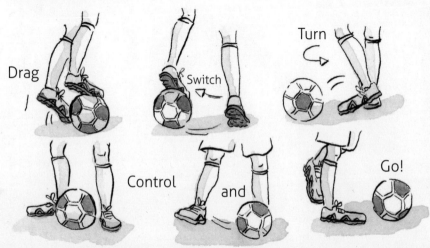

Drag   Switch   Turn

Control   and   Go!

SPOT THE DIFFERENCE!

Can you find the ten differences
between the two pictures?

Why are wingers so cool? Because they stand nearest the fans!
What never moves but runs the whole length of the pitch? The sideline!
What's the best thing to do when the pitch floods? Bring on your subs!
When fish play football, who is the captain? The team's kipper!
MR AZIZ'S FOOTBALL JOKES

GRAB THE WHISTLE

1. A player gets so excited during his goal celebration that he rips his top off.
What do you do?
a) Show him a yellow card
b) Lend him your own strip
c) Disallow the goal

> If you were the referee, would you make the right call?

2. A player answers their phone on the pitch. What do you do?
a) Blow the whistle and ask the other players to be quiet until they're done
b) Send the player off
c) Book them for unsporting behaviour

3. A player throws the ball from a throw-in straight to their keeper, who catches it.
What do you do?
a) Sigh and ask the goalkeeper to throw it back
b) Award the throw-in to the opposing team
c) Give the opposing team an indirect free kick from where the keeper caught it

Answers: 1a, 2c, 3c